M.J.Hümmel®

Christmas

Angels

Dutton Children's Books

NEW YORK

$\mathscr{A}$ friend is an angel who knows the song in your heart
and can sing it back to you when you have forgotten the words.

—ANONYMOUS

$\mathcal{B}$e welcoming to strangers: for those who have done so
have sometimes entertained angels unawares.

—HEBREWS 13:2

There were some shepherds staying out in the fields and keeping watch over their flock by night. And an angel of the Lord suddenly stood before them, and the glory of the Lord shone around them; and they were terribly frightened. But the angel said to them, "Do not be afraid; for behold, I bring you good news of great joy which will be for all the people; for today in the city of David there has been born for you a Savior, who is Christ the Lord."

—LUKE 2:8–11

4

For every soul, there is a guardian watching it.
—THE KORAN

*I*f instead of a gem, or even a flower, we should
cast the gift of a loving thought into the heart of
a friend, that would be giving as the angels give.

—GEORGE MACDONALD

Be Thy right hand, O God, under my head,
Be Thy light, O Spirit, over me shining.
And be the cross of the nine angels over me down,
From the crown of my head to the soles of my feet,
From the crown of my head to the soles of my feet.

—ANCIENT CELTIC PRAYER

Angels bless and angels keep,
Angels guard me while I sleep.
Bless my heart and bless my home,
Bless my spirit as I roam.
Guide and guard me through the night
And wake me with the morning's light.

—AUTHOR UNKNOWN

$\mathcal{L}$ord, keep us safe this night,
Secure from all our fears;
May angels guard us while we sleep,
Till morning light appears.

—JOHN LELAND

$\mathcal{K}$eep us, O Lord, as the apple of your eye;
Hide us under the shadow of your wings.

—THE BOOK OF COMMON PRAYER

Dear Angel ever at my side,
how lovely you must be
to leave your home in heaven
to guard a child like me.
When I am far away from home,
or maybe hard at play,
I know you will protect me
from harm along the way.
Your beautiful and shining face,
I see not, though you're near.
The sweetness of your lovely voice,
I cannot really hear.
When I pray, you're praying too;
your prayer is just for me.
But when I sleep, you never do—
you're watching over me.

—AUTHOR UNKNOWN

$\mathcal{T}$o love for the sake of being loved is human,
but to love for the sake of loving is angelic.
—ALPHONSE DE LAMARTINE

The guardian angels of life sometimes
fly so high as to be beyond our sight,
but they are always looking down upon us.
—JEAN PAUL RICHTER

Silently one by one, in the infinite meadows of Heaven,
Blossomed the lovely stars, the forget-me-nots of the Angels.

—HENRY WADSWORTH LONGFELLOW

✺

We are each of us angels with only one wing,
And we can only fly by embracing each other.

—LUCIANO DE CRESCENZO

✺

The golden moments in the stream of life rush past us,
and we see nothing but sand; the angels come to visit us,
and we only know them when they are gone.

—GEORGE ELIOT

The fire upon the hearth is low,
And there is stillness everywhere,
And, like winged spirits, here and there
The firelight shadows fluttering go.
—EUGENE FIELD

Music is well said to be the speech of angels.

—THOMAS CARLYLE

Sleep, my child, and peace attend thee,
All through the night.
Guardian angels God will send thee,
All through the night.
Soft the drowsy hours are creeping,
Hill and vale in slumber sleeping,
I my loving vigil keeping,
All through the night.

   —SIR HAROLD BOULTON

   (BASED ON A WELSH FOLK SONG)

Angel of God, my guardian dear,
To whom God's love commits me here,
Ever this day be at my side,
To light and guard, to rule and guide.

—TRADITIONAL

CIP Data is available.

Published in the United States by Dutton Children's Books,
a division of Penguin Young Readers Group
345 Hudson Street, New York, New York 10014
www.penguin.com

Manufactured in China · Designed by Tim Hall
ISBN 0-525-47309-2
First Edition
1 3 5 7 9 10 8 6 4 2